The Giant Crab
And Other Tales
from Old India

Retold by
W. H. D. Rouse

Illustrated by W. Robinson

London
David Nutt, 270-271, Strand
1897

I

The Pious Wolf

The Giant Crab

And Other Tales from Old India

Retold by
W. H. D. Rouse
Illustrated by W. Robinson

Warning

To the Studious or Scientific Reader

I hope no one will imagine this to be a scientific book. It is meant to amuse children; and if it succeeds in this, its aim will be hit. Thus the stories here given, although grounded upon the great Buddhist collection named below, have been ruthlessly altered wherever this would better suit them for the purpose in view; and probably some of them Buddha himself would fail to recognise.

My thanks are due to the Syndics of the Cambridge University Press for permitting the use of their translation of the *Jātaka Book*,[1] from which comes the groundwork of the stories, and occasionally a phrase or a versicle is borrowed. To this work I refer all scholars, folk-lorists and scientific persons generally: warning them that if they plunge deeper into these pages, they will be horribly shocked.

---

[1] The *Jātaka*; or Stories of the Buddha's former Births. Translated from the Pāli by various hands, under the editorship of Professor E. B. Cowell. Vol. I., translated by R. Chalmers, B.A. (1895). Vol. II., translated by W. H. D. Rouse, M.A. (1895). Vol. III., translated by H. T. Francis, M.A., and R. A. Neil, M.A. (1897). Vol. IV., in preparation. All the stories but two come from the second volume of this work.

Contents

The Giant Crab

Once upon a time there was a lake in the mountains, and in that lake lived a huge Crab. I daresay you have often seen crabs boiled, and put on a dish for you to eat; and perhaps at the seaside you have watched them sidling away at the bottom of a pool. Sometimes a boy or girl bathing in the sea gets a nip from a crab, and then there is squeaking and squealing. But our Crab was much larger than these; he was the largest Crab ever heard of; he was bigger than a dining-room table, and his claws were as big as an armchair. Fancy what it must be to have a nip from such claws as those!

Well, this huge Crab lived all alone in the lake. Now the different animals that lived in the wild mountains used to come to that lake to drink; deer and antelopes, foxes and wolves, lions and tigers and elephants. And whenever they came into the water to drink, the great Crab was on the watch; and one of them at least never went up out of the water again. The Crab used to nip it with one of his huge claws and pull it under, and then the poor beast was drowned, and made a fine dinner for the big Crab.

This went on for a long time, and the Crab grew bigger and bigger every day, fattening on the animals that came there to drink. So at last all the animals were afraid to go near that lake. This was a pity, because there was very little water in the mountains, and the creatures did not know what to do when they were thirsty.

At last a great Elephant made up his mind to put an end to the Crab and his doings. So he and his wife agreed that they would lead a herd of elephants there to drink, and while the other elephants were drinking, they would look out for the Crab.

They did as they arranged. When the herd of elephants got to the lake, these two went in first, and kept farthest out in the water, watching for the Crab; and the others drank, and trumpeted, and washed themselves close inshore.

Soon they had had enough, and began to go out of the water; and then, sure enough, the Elephant felt a tremendous nip on the leg. The Crab had crawled up under the water and got him fast. He nodded to his wife, who bravely stayed by his side; and then she began:

"Dear Mr. Crab!" she said, "please let my husband go!"

The Crab poked his eyes out of the water. You know a crab's eyes grow on a kind of little stalk; and this Crab was so big, that his eyes looked like two thick tree-trunks, with a cannon-ball on the top of each. Now this Crab was a great flirt, or rather he used to be a great flirt, but lately he had nobody to flirt with, because he had eaten up all the creatures that came near him. And Mrs. Elephant was a beautiful elephant, with a shiny brown skin, and elegant flapping ears, and a curly trunk, and two white tusks that twinkled when she smiled. So when the big Crab saw this beautiful elephant, he thought he would like to have a kiss; and he said in a wheedling tone:

"Dear little Elephant! Will you give me a kiss?"

Then Mrs. Elephant pretended to be very pleased, and put her head on one side, and flapped her tail; and she looked so sweet and so tempting, that the Crab let go the other elephant, and began to crawl slowly towards her, waving his eyes about as he went.

All this while Mr. Elephant had been in great pain from the nip of the Crab's claw, but he had said nothing, for he was a very brave Elephant. But he did not mean to let his wife come to any harm; not he! It was all part of their trick. And as soon as he felt his leg free, he trumpeted loud and long, and jumped right upon the Crab's back!

Crack, crack! went the Crab's shell; for, big as he was, an elephant was too heavy for him to carry. Crack, crack, crack! The Elephant jumped up and down on his back, and in a very short time the Crab was crushed to mincemeat.

What rejoicing there was among the animals when they saw the Crab crushed to death! From far and near they came, and passed a vote of thanks to the Elephant and his wife, and made them King and Queen of all the animals in the mountains.

As for the Crab, there was nothing left of him but his claws, which were so hard that nothing could even crack them; so they were left in the pool. And in the autumn there came a great flood, and carried the claws down into the river; and the river carried them hundreds of miles away, to a great city; where the King's sons found them, and made out of them two immense drums, which they always beat when they go to war; and the very sound of these drums is enough to frighten the enemy away.

The Hypocritical Cat

Once upon a time there was a troop of Rats that used to live in holes by a river side. A certain Cat often saw them going to and fro, and longed to have them to eat. But he was not strong enough to attack them all together; besides, that would not have suited his purpose, because most of them would have run away.

So he used to stand early in the morning, not far from their holes, with his face towards the sun, snuffing up the air, and standing on one leg.

The Rats wondered why he did that, so one day they all trooped up to him in a body, and asked the reason.

"What is your name, sir?" they began.

"Holy is my name," said the Cat.

"Why do you stand on one leg?"

"Because if I stood on all four, the earth could not bear my weight."

"And why do you keep your mouth open?"

"Because I feed on the air, and never eat anything else."

"And why do you face the sun?"

"Because I worship the sun."

"What a pious Cat!" the Rats all thought. Ever after that, when they started out in the morning, they did not fail first to make their bow to the Cat one by one, and to show thus their respect for his piety.

This was just what our Cat wanted. Every day, as they filed past, he waited till the tail of the string came up; then like lightning pounced upon the hindmost, and gobbled him up in a trice; after which he stood on one leg as before, licking his lips greedily.

For a while all went well for the Cat's plan; but at last the Chief of the Rats noticed that the troop seemed to grow smaller. Here and there he missed some familiar face. He could not make it out; but at last a thought came into his mind, that perhaps the pious Cat might know more about it than he chose to tell.

Next day accordingly, he posted himself at the tail of the troop, where he could see everything that went on; and as the Rats one by one bowed before the Cat, he watched the Cat out of the end of his eye.

As he came up, the Cat prepared for his pounce. But our Rat was ready for him, and dodged out of the way.

"Aha!" says the Rat, "so that is your piety! Feeds on the air, does he! and worships the sun—eh? What a humbug!" And with one spring he was at the Cat's throat, and his sharp teeth fast. The other Rats heard the scuffle, and came trooping back; and it was crunch and munch, till not a vestige remained of the hypocritical Cat. Those who came first had cat to eat, and those who came last went sniffing about at the mouths of their friends, and asking what was the taste of catsmeat. And ever after the Rats lived in peace and happiness.

The Crocodile and the Monkey

Once upon a time there was a deep and wide river, and in this river lived a crocodile. I do not know whether you have ever seen a crocodile; but if you did see one, I am sure you would be frightened. They are very long, twice as long as your bed; and they are covered with hard green or yellow scales; and they have a wide flat snout, and a huge jaw with hundreds of sharp teeth, so big that it could hold you all at once inside it. This crocodile used to lie all day in the mud, half under water, basking in the sun, and never moving; but if any little animal came near, he would jump up, and open his big jaws, and snap it up as a dog snaps up a fly. And if you had gone near him, he would have snapped you up too, just as easily.

On the bank of this river lived a monkey. He spent the day climbing about the trees, and eating nuts or wild fruit; but he had been there so long, that there was hardly any fruit left upon the trees.

Now it so happened that the crocodile's wife cast a longing eye on this Monkey. She was very dainty in her eating, was Mrs. Crocodile, and she liked the tit-bits. So one morning she began to cry. Crocodile's tears are very big, and as her tears dropped into the water, splash, splash, splash, Mr. Crocodile woke up from his snooze, and looked round to see what was the matter.

"Why, wife," said he, "what are you crying about?"

"I'm hungry!" whimpered Mrs. Crocodile.

"All right," said he, "wait a while. I'll soon catch you something."

"But I want that Monkey's heart!" said Mrs. Crocodile. Splash, splash, splash, went her tears again.

"Come, come, cheer up," said Mr. Crocodile. He was very fond of his wife, and he would have wiped away her tears, only he had no pocket-handkerchief. "Cheer up!" said he; "I'll see what I can do."

His wife dried her tears, and Mr. Crocodile lay down again on the mud, thinking. He thought for a whole hour. You see, though he was very big, he was very stupid. At last he heaved a sigh of relief, for he thought he had hit upon a clever plan.

He wallowed along the bank to a place just underneath a big tree. Up on the tree our Monkey was swinging by his tail, and chattering to himself.

"Monkey!" he called out, in the softest voice he could manage. It was not very soft, something like a policeman's rattle; but it was the best he could do, with all those sharp teeth.

The Monkey stopped swinging, and looked down. The Crocodile had never spoken to him before, and he felt rather surprised.

"Monkey, dear!" called the Crocodile, again.

"Well, what is it?" asked the Monkey.

"I'm sure you must be hungry," said Mr. Crocodile. "I see you have eaten all the fruit on these trees; but why don't you try the trees on the other side of the river? Just look, apples, pears, quinces, plums, anything you could wish for! And heaps of them!"

"That is all very well," said the Monkey. "But how can I get across a wide river like this?"

"Oh!" said the cunning Crocodile, "that is easily managed. I like your looks, and I want to do you a good turn. Jump on my back, and I'll swim across; then you can enjoy yourself!"

Never had the Monkey had an offer so tempting. He swung round a branch three times in his joy; his eyes glistened, and without thinking a moment, down he jumped on the Crocodile's back.

The Crocodile began to swim slowly across. The Monkey fixed his eyes on the opposite bank with its glorious fruit trees, and danced for joy. Suddenly he felt the water about his feet! It rose to his legs, it rose to his middle. The Crocodile was sinking!

"Mr. Crocodile! Mr. Crocodile! take care!" said he. "You'll drown me!"

"Ha, ha, ha!" laughed the Crocodile, snapping his great jaws. "So you thought I was taking you across out of pure good nature! You are a green monkey, to be sure. The truth is, my wife has taken a fancy to you, and wants your heart to eat! If you had seen her crying this morning, I am sure you would have pitied her."

"What a good thing you told me!" said the Monkey. (He was a very clever Monkey, and had his wits about him.) "Wait a bit, and I'll tell you why. My heart, I think you said? Why, I never carry my heart inside me; that would be too dangerous. If we Monkeys went jumping about the trees with our hearts inside, we should knock them to bits in no time."

The Crocodile rose up to the surface again. He felt very glad he had not drowned the Monkey, because, as I said, he was a stupid creature, and did not see that the Monkey was playing him a trick.

"Oh," said he, "where is your heart, then?"

"Do you see that cluster of round things up in the tree there, on the further bank? Those are our hearts, all in a bunch; and pretty safe too, at that height, I should hope!" It was really a fig-tree, and certainly the figs did look very much like a bunch of hearts. "Just you take me across," he went on, "and I'll climb up and drop my heart down; I can do very well without it."

"You excellent creature!" said the Crocodile, "so I will!"

And he swam across the river. The Monkey leapt lightly off the Crocodile's back, and swung himself up the fig-tree. Then he sat down on a branch, and began to eat the figs with great enjoyment.

"Your heart, please!" called out the Crocodile. "Can't you see I'm waiting?"

"Well, wait as long as you like!" said the Monkey. "Are you such a fool as to think that any creature keeps its heart in a tree? Your body is big, but your wit is little. No, no; here I am, and here I mean to stay. Many thanks for bringing me over!"

The Crocodile snapped his jaws in disgust, and went back to his wife, feeling very foolish, as he was; and the Monkey had such a feast in the fig-tree as he never had in his life before.

The Axe, the Drum, the Bowl, and the Diamond

Once upon a time there was a poor young man who went out into the world to seek his fortune. He went aboard a ship sailing across the ocean; and after they had sailed for a year and a day, suddenly a great storm arose. The rain descended, and the wind blew, and it blew so hard and so wild, that the ship went miles out of her course, and the skipper could not tell where they were. And then, in the middle of the night, a great crash came, and the ship was dashed upon a reef. The waves beat and battered it, and turned it topsy-turvy, and the end of it was that every soul was drowned except the poor young man.

The waves washed him ashore, more dead than alive, and on the shore he lay till next morning, when the sun warmed him and woke him up from his faint. He got up and looked about him, and wandered over the place, which he found was an island. It did not take him long to walk round it; and then he saw that it was a small island, and far as the eye could reach not another speck of land was to be seen. There were plenty of trees growing in the island, with fruit and flowers, bananas and cocoanuts, and springs of water; but on the trees were no birds, and no animals ran about on the ground. So he lived on the fruits and roots, and did the best he could.

One day, to his great surprise, he saw a black thing in the sky; and, still more surprising, the black thing had no wings. Yet it was flying, and flew nearer and nearer, until he saw that it was a large wild pig. How could a pig fly through the air? He rubbed his eyes and looked again; yes, a pig it was beyond all doubt; and it flew closer and closer until it came to the island. He hid behind a bush, and saw the pig sink slowly to the ground and lie down under a tree. Soon the pig was fast asleep and snoring. He went up close, and, to his amazement, by the pig's side, was the most magnificent diamond he ever saw. It blazed and sparkled in the sun and looked like a ball of fire. He stepped gingerly up to the pig, and took hold of the diamond; the pig was very sleepy and snored away heartily. As he turned the diamond about in his hand and saw it flash, he suddenly thought to himself, "What if the pig should wake? He looks fierce, he has great sharp tusks, and I have nothing to defend myself with. If I were only up in that tree, now——" But what on earth had happened? As the thought came into his mind, he found himself perched in the tree-top.

For a little while he was quite dazed and dizzy. Then he began to wonder if it could be the diamond which had done this miracle. So just to try, he wished himself down again; and there he was, without knowing how! He began to understand that this was a magic diamond, and something which he must take great care of. Then he wished himself up in the tree again.

When he was in the tree once more, he picked off a nut that was growing on the tree, and dropped it upon the pig's nose. The pig woke up, raised his head, and looked round for the diamond; he was a very intelligent pig, indeed he was really not a pig at all, but a great magician, who used to fly about in the shape of a pig because he was as wicked as could be, and preferred being a pig rather than a man. There are really a great many people like that, only we see them in the shape of men and do not know the difference.

Now when this pig saw that his diamond was gone, he fell in a fury; for all his power lay in the diamond, and without it he was nothing more than any other pig. So he glared and snorted, and looked all round, and down, and up—and then he saw the man who had dropped the nut upon his snout! Then his fury knew no bounds; he foamed at the mouth, and ran raging round and round the tree; but the man only laughed, and dropped more nuts on him. This made him mad indeed, for pigs cannot climb trees, and he saw that his diamond was lost, and with it all his magical power; so in his madness he charged straight at the tree, and ran his tusks right into the trunk. There they stuck, and tug as he would, he could not get them out.

The man wished himself down from the tree, and looked about for a large stone, with which he battered the pig's skull till it was dead. Then he held the diamond over the pig, so that the sun's rays shone down and were reflected through it; and so fine and strong was the diamond, that in a very short time a delicious smell of roast pork rose to his nostrils, and the whole pig was done to a turn, with rich crisp crackling. Then he took a sharp shell which he found lying on the beach, and carved off slices of the pork, which he ate. It was very nice indeed, and he had the best meal he had enjoyed since the ship had been wrecked on the reef, and he had been cast ashore on that island.

By-and-by, when he had finished his dinner, it occurred to him that as the pig had flown there through the air, so he might fly away. So holding his diamond in his hand, he wished to fly through the air to the nearest land. Then he felt himself rising, and he was carried swiftly through the air, and away, away over the sea; the island grew smaller, it became a black patch, it dwindled to a speck in the distance. The sun shone warm upon him, the waves sparkled underneath; porpoises gambolled about, playing leap-frog in the sea; flying-fish came out of the water in a flash of light, and dropped into the water again; still he went on, till, as the sun was setting, he came close to a sandy beach; and there before long he stood, wondering what he should do next.

He looked round, and not far off, behind a clump of bushes, rose a thin column of smoke. He put the diamond in his pocket, and walked towards the smoke. Soon he saw a queer little hut, and at the door, upon the ground, sat a man without any legs. Whether a shark had bitten off his legs, or whether he never had any, I cannot tell you, for he never told me; but there he sat, like a chessman. He had a fur cap, and a fur coat; he did not need any trousers, for he had no legs to put them on, as I have told you. In front of him was a fire, and over the fire was a spit, and on the spit was a young kid roasting.

"Good evening, sir," said the young man.

"Good evening," said the other.

"Can you give me a night's shelter?" the young man asked.

"Whatever I have, you may share," said the old man with no legs.

So they sat down, and ate a good meal; but the young man was rather frightened to see that the other man ate skin, and bones, and everything. And he did not like the way the old man eyed him. In fact I must tell you, that this old man was another magician, and a friend of the magician who looked like a pig; and when any travellers came that way, he used to eat them. He did not eat this traveller, because the kid was ready roasted; but he meant to do it as soon as he should be hungry again.

"How did you get here?" asked the old man.

"I flew over the sea," said the young man.

"Indeed!" said the old man. "And how did you manage that?"

Then the traveller showed his diamond, and told the old man what a wonderful stone it was, and how it gave any one power to fly through the air.

"If you will give me your diamond," said the old man, "I will give you my axe. You see I have no legs, so you may wonder how I live. This is the way I live. If I slap this axe on the handle, and say, Wood and fire! away it flies, and cuts wood and kindles a fire. If I slap the steel, and say, Heads! away it flies, and chops off the head of a goat or any animal I want; and then it brings me meat for my dinner. Now I have lived here for a thousand years by the help of my axe, and I am rather tired of being in one place. I should like to see the world before I die, and that is why I want your diamond."

"All right," said the young man, "it's a bargain." They exchanged the axe and the diamond; the old man turned it over in his hand, chuckling greedily. As soon as the young man got grip of the axe, he smacked the steel, and says he, "Heads!" In a jiffy the axe sliced through the old man's neck like a turnip, and he had no more head than legs.

Then the traveller picked up the diamond, and put it in his pocket. So now he had two magic things instead of one. He blessed his luck, and fell asleep very happily inside the old magician's hut.

Next morning, with the diamond in his pocket and the axe on his shoulder, the young man set out on his travels. All day long he walked through the forest, until at evening time he saw before him another hut, like the first, where lived the old man with no legs. Before this hut, too, there was a fire burning, and beside the fire sat an old man without any arms. Whether a tiger had bitten off his arms or whether he never had any, I cannot say, because he never told me; but there he sat like a pair of compasses. He had the stump of a tree to sit on, and before him was another stump, and on this stump was a large bowl of milk, out of which he was drinking. When he saw our friend, he tipped over this bowl with his chin; instantly a deep roaring river surrounded him and his hut, and he sat in the middle, laughing at the young man's surprise. But he did not laugh long, for the young man instantly wished himself over the river, and there he was. Now it was his turn to laugh.

"How on earth did you do that?" asked the old man. He was much too astonished to think of saying good-day.

"Oh, that's nothing," said the young man, and showed him his diamond.

The old man's eyes glistened. He thought how nice it would be to have that diamond.

"What do you say to selling me that diamond?" said he.

"What will you give me for it?" asked the young man.

"I will give you this bowl. It is a wishing bowl. Whenever you are hungry all you have to do is to wish for something in it, and there it is; milk, or soup, or wine; anything that can go in a bowl. And if you turn it over, as you saw me do just now, a rushing, roaring river pours out, and surrounds you, or, if you like, it will flood a whole country and drown every living thing."

"Dear me!" said the young man, "that is a wonderful bowl. Well, I agree; I'll give you my diamond for it." So they exchanged the bowl and the diamond. The old man took the diamond in his hand and watched it sparkle; but he did not watch long, for the young man slapped his hatchet and cried, "Heads!" In a jiffy the steel sliced through the old man's neck like a cucumber, and he had no more head than arms. Then the young man picked up his diamond and put it away in his pocket. So now he had three wonderful things instead of two. He blessed his good luck, wished for some delicious wine in his bowl, drank it, and went to sleep happily, in the old man's hut.

Next morning the young man was up betimes; and after taking a meal out of his wishing-bowl, he set out once more to walk through the forest. After he had walked for some hours, he heard, far in the distance, a loud rub-a-dub-dub, rub-a-dub-dub, boom, boom, boom. He felt as if he could hardly help running away; still, with a great effort, he began to walk towards the sound, which got louder and louder every minute, till at last it made a tremendous din. Then, suddenly, just as he came upon a little open glade in the forest, he heard a rustle, bustle, jostle, and out of the trees came a great herd of elephants, lions, tigers, wolves, and all sorts of wild animals, their hair bristling with fright, and every one of them tearing along at full speed. They were far too much terrified to notice him, and, scurrying across the glade, they vanished among the trees.

By this time the noise had ceased, but it was not long before he came upon another little glade, and at the end of the glade was a hut, and in front of that hut sat a big black giant with a drum.

"Good day to you!" roared the giant, in a great voice.

"Good day!" said the young man, rather frightened.

"Come and have something to eat!" roared the giant.

"Thank you," said the young man.

They sat down, and the giant offered him some food. But the young man thought it was safer not to take any of the giant's food, so he pulled out his bowl, and wished for some soup, and sipped it.

27

"What is that?" asked the giant.

The young man told him it was a wishing bowl, that gave any food he wanted. The giant was very much delighted with the wishing bowl, and thought that if he could get that bowl, he would be able to eat without the trouble of getting things.

"I'll buy that bowl!" he roared.

"What will you give me for it?" asked the young man.

"I will give you this drum," said the giant. "If you beat on one side, everybody that hears it will run away."

"Ah, that was why the lions and tigers were running away just now!" said the young man.

"Yes," said the giant. "And if you beat on the other side, a splendid army of soldiers and horses will spring up out of the ground and defend you."

"All right, here you are," said the young man, and gave him the bowl.

The giant took the bowl in great glee, and horrid to tell, wished out loud for a bowlful of blood! He began to drink it, but he did not finish; for as he buried his nose in the bowl, the young man slapped his axe, and said—"Heads!" Down came the axe with a crash on the giant's head, and cut it clean in two!

If the young man was glad when he saw the giant's head cleft in two, he was gladder when he went inside the giant's hut. For there, all round the wall, were the bodies of travellers who had passed that way; and they were tied to the uprights of the wall, and their bodies were dry as dust, and shrivelled like a medlar. For this giant used to catch all travellers and tie them up in his house, and then he sucked their blood till they were dry. So when our traveller saw what a narrow escape he had had, he determined no longer to remain in that dreadful place. Picking up the bowl and the drum, and feeling to see that his axe and diamond were safe, he wished himself at the gate of the nearest city.

Now the king of this city was a very cruel king. He used to rob and murder even his own subjects; and as for strangers, he had short shrift and no mercy for them. So when the king heard that there was a stranger outside the gates, he made up his mind to have some sport; and sent out a company of soldiers to fetch him in. The young man beat his drum, and they all took to their heels! You may imagine how angry the king was to hear this; he had all their heads chopped off on the spot, and sent a regiment. The same thing happened to the regiment. But this only made the king angrier than ever. He ordered all his army to be marshalled before the gates, and himself riding at their head, led them forward to capture this audacious stranger. Then the young man tipped over his wishing bowl. Out poured a roaring torrent of water that flooded the plain, and drowned every soldier in the army, all except the king, who had galloped back to the city, and got up on the wall. Then the young man slapped his axe, and cried, "Heads! I want the king's head!" Off flew the axe through the air like a boomerang, and sliced off the king's head, and brought it back to its master. The people inside the city began to cheer with joy, when they saw the king with his head off. And when the axe came back, the young man beat upon the other side of his drum; and lo and behold! the earth began to tremble, it seemed full of holes, and from every hole sprouted a warrior fully armed. Surrounded by his army, he marched into the city, where he became king, and lived happily ever after. And I hope that we may be half as happy as he was.

The Wise Parrot and the Foolish Parrot

Once upon a time there was a man who had two pet parrots that could talk very nicely; indeed they had more sense than most people have, and when their master was alone he used to spend the evening chattering with them. They cracked jokes like any Christian, and told the funniest tales.

But this man had a thievish maid-servant. He had to lock everything up, and even as it was, never turned his back but she was filching and pilfering.

One day the man had to go away on a journey. Before he went he took out the two parrots, and perched one on each fist, and says he to them, "Now, Beaky and Tweaky, I want you to watch the maid while I am gone; and if she steals anything, you are to tell me when I come home again."

They blinked at him, their eyelids coming up over their eyes from underneath, as you must have noticed in parrots; looking very solemn as they did so. Then Beaky said,

"If she do it
She shall rue it!"

But Tweaky said nothing at all; only winked again more solemnly than ever.

"Good Beaky!" said the man, "naughty Tweaky!"

Then he went away.

As soon as he was out of sight, the maid began her games. She picked the locks of his cupboards and ate the sugar, she ate the biscuits, she drank the wine. Beaky hopped into the room, stood on one leg, and shrieked,

"Naughty maid!
Aren't you afraid?
Master shall know,
And you shall go!"

The maid jumped as if she had been shot, and looked round. She thought somebody had caught her unawares; but when she saw it was Beaky she put on a sweet smile, and held out a lump of sugar, saying in a coaxing voice, "Pretty Poll! pretty Beaky! I won't do it again! Come, then, and have a nice lump of sugar."

This temptation was too strong for poor Beaky. He wanted very much to do his duty, but he wanted the lump of sugar more. So he put his head on one side and, looking very wise, sidled up to the maid. This was very wrong of Beaky, because he knew the sugar was stolen; and in another minute he was sorry; for as soon as he came within reach and pecked at the sugar, the maid caught him by the neck with the other hand. Then her smile changed, and she sneered,

"So Beaky is going to tell, is he? Tell-tale tit! I'll teach Beaky to tell tales!" As she said each word, she plucked out a feather from poor Beaky's head. Beaky shrieked and Beaky struggled, but all in vain; she did not let him go till he was bald as a bullet.

Tweaky saw all this, but said nothing, only winked and blinked, and looked more solemn than ever. The maid looked at him, but thought she, "That bird is too stupid to tell, and he isn't worth the trouble of plucking." So she left him alone.

By-and-by the master came in. The maid went up to him in a great bustle, and said she had found Beaky stealing sugar, and she had plucked him as a punishment.

When the evening came, the master sat in his room with Beaky and Tweaky. Poor Beaky felt ashamed of himself, and had nothing to say; he sat on his perch the picture of misery, with his tail drooping, and his ridiculous bald head. Tweaky said nothing at all.

Now it happened that the master had a bald head too, and when he took off his skull-cap, which he generally wore to keep his head warm, Tweaky noticed it.

He laughed loud and shrieked out, "Oh-oh-oh! Where's your feathers, Tell-tale tit? Where's your feathers, Tell-tale tit?"

Tweaky was only a parrot, you see, and was not always quite correct in his grammar, as you are.

"What do you mean?" asked the master.

But for a long time Tweaky would say nothing but the same words over and over again, "Where's your feathers, Tell-tale tit?" However, by-and-by they heard the maid going to bed, tramp, tramp, tramp. Then Tweaky grew a little braver; and next time the master asked him what he meant, he replied:

"Every parrot has two eyes,
Both the foolish and the wise;
But the wise can shut them tight
When 'tis best to have no sight.
Wisdom has the best of it:
Where's your feathers, Tell-tale tit?"

Then the master understood what had happened, for he was a very clever man; and without any delay he ran upstairs two steps at a time, and woke the maid, and made her dress herself, and turned her out of the house then and there. I wonder why he did not do it before, but that is no business of mine.

After that, poor Beaky never had the heart to talk again; but Tweaky, whenever he saw a bald-headed man, or a woman with a high forehead, shrieked out at the top of his voice—

"Ha! ha! ha! Where's your feathers, Tell-tale tit?"

The Dishonest Friend

There was once a man who went on a journey, and he asked a friend to take charge of his plough till he should return. The friend promised to take great care of it. But no sooner was the man gone than he sold the plough and put the price in his own pocket. Was not that a mean trick to serve a friend?

The man came back, and asked his friend for the plough.

"Oh, I am so sorry," the friend replied; "my house is infested with rats, and one night a very big rat came and ate it up."

"Ah well," said the man, "what can't be cured must be endured! It must have been a very big rat, though."

"It was," said the other, "very big."

You must not suppose this man was quite such a fool as he seemed. You will soon see why he did not make a fuss about his plough.

Next day he took his friend's son out for a walk. When they had gone some distance he took the boy to another friend's house, and told this friend to keep the boy safe, but not to let him go out of the house till he returned.

Then he ran back to the boy's father.

"Where is my boy?" asked the father.

"Your boy? Oh, I remember—a hawk swooped down and carried him off."

"Oh, you liar! oh, you murderer!" said the friend. "Come before the judge, and then we shall see."

"As you please," said the man.

So they went to the court.

"What is your complaint?" asked the judge.

"My lord, this man took my son out for a walk with him, and came back alone, and now he says a hawk carried him off. He must have murdered the boy! Justice, my lord, justice!"

"What is this?" asked the judge sternly. "Come, my man, tell the truth."

"It is the truth, my lord," said the man; "he came with me for a walk, and was carried away by a hawk."

"Nonsense!" said the judge. "Who ever heard of a hawk carrying off a boy?"

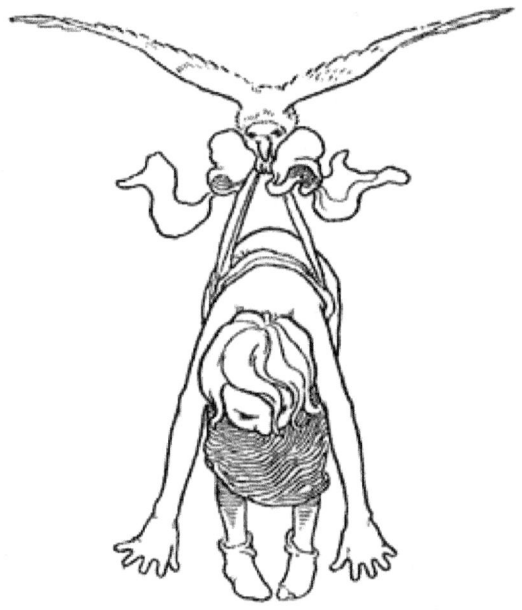

"And who ever heard, my lord, of a rat eating a plough?"

"What do you mean?" asked the judge.

The man told his story. Then the judge saw that the man who complained had cheated his friend, and understood what was the reason of this little trick. So he said to the man whose son was lost:

"If you find the plough that was entrusted to you, perhaps your son may be found too."

The man was much annoyed at being found out, but, willy nilly, he had to give the plough back. Then his son was brought back safe to him again. And he began to see that honesty is the best policy.

The Mouse and the Farmer

Once upon a time there was a Mouse, who made his hole in a place where there were thousands and thousands of golden sovereigns buried in the ground. Now there was a Farmer who owned the land where this treasure was buried; but he did not know about it, or else of course he would have dug it up. He often noticed the little Mouse sitting with his head peeping out of the hole, but as he was a very kind Farmer, he never hurt the Mouse; and now and then when he was having his own dinner, he would throw the Mouse a bit of cheese.

The Mouse was very grateful to the Farmer, and wondered what he could do to show it. At last he thought of the treasure; for this Mouse was sensible enough to know that Farmers are very pleased to get a golden sovereign now and again. So one day, as the Farmer went by the hole, Mousie ran out with a golden sovereign in his mouth, and dropped it at the Farmer's feet. You can imagine how glad the Farmer was to see a golden sovereign. Indeed, it was the first one he had seen since the Corn Laws were abolished. So he thanked the Mouse, and went down to the village, and bought him a beautiful piece of meat. After this the Mouse every day brought the Farmer a golden sovereign, and every day the Farmer gave him a big chunk of meat. Thus in a few weeks Mousie grew quite fat.

But the Farmer had a big black cat that used to prowl about watching for mice. It used never to notice the Farmer's own favourite Mouse while the Mouse was thin; but when he grew sleek and fat and shiny, Grimalkin (which was the Cat's name) lay in wait for him one day and pounced upon him. Poor little Mousie was terrified.

"Please don't kill me, Mr. Grimalkin!" said Mousie.

"Why not? I'm hungry and you are fat!"

"But, sir, if you eat me now, you'll be hungry to-morrow, won't you?"

"Of course I shall!" said Grimalkin.

"Well," said Mousie, who had suddenly thought of a plan; "if you will only let me go, I'll bring you a beautiful juicy piece of meat every day!"

This was a tempting offer for Grimalkin, who was a lazy Cat, and liked sitting by the fire, and licking himself all over, better than hunting for mice.

"All right," said he; "only if you leave out one day, you're a dead mouse!" Then, with a frightful spit, bristling up all his whiskers and eyebrows, Grimalkin ran away.

So next day, when the Farmer gave Mousie his dinner, Mousie carried it off to the black Cat, and the black Cat spat and swore and ate it up, and away ran Mousie trembling. But by degrees Mousie grew thinner and thinner, because Grimalkin always had his dinner; and soon he was nothing but skin and bone. Then the Farmer noticed how thin his Mouse had become, so one day he asked the Mouse whether he was ill.

"No," said Mousie, "I'm not ill."

"What is the matter, then?" asked the Farmer.

"I never get any dinner now," said Mousie, with tears running down over his nose, "because Grimalkin eats it all!" Then he told the Farmer about the bargain he had made with Grimalkin.

Now the Farmer had a beautiful piece of glass, with a hole in the middle. I think it was an inkstand, but I am not sure. So he took this piece of glass and put Mousie inside it, and turned it upside down upon the ground in front of Mousie's hole. "Now," said he, "next time Grimalkin comes for your dinner, tell him you have none for him, and see what will happen."

So next day up comes Grimalkin for his dinner, spitting and looking very fierce.

"Meat! meat!" says he to the Mouse.

"Get off, vile thief!" says Mousie, "I've no meat for the likes of you!"

At this Grimalkin could hardly believe his ears. He was in a rage, I can tell you; and, without stopping to think, pounced upon Mousie, and swallowed him, inkstand and all. You see, as it was all glass, Grimalkin did not know that there was any inkstand there, because he saw the Mouse through it.

Now cats can digest a good deal, but they can't digest a glass inkstand. So Grimalkin, when he had swallowed the Mouse and the inkstand, felt a pain inside; and this got worse and worse, until at last he died. And then Mousie crept out of the inkstand, and crawled up through Grimalkin's throat, and went back to his hole again. And there he lived all his life in happiness, every day bringing a golden sovereign to the Farmer, who gave him every day a beautiful dinner of meat.

The Talkative Tortoise

Once upon a time there was a Tortoise that lived in a pond. He was a most worthy Tortoise, but he had one fault, he would talk in season and out of season; all day long it was chatter, chatter, chatter in that pond, until the fish said that they would rather live on dry land than put up with it any longer.

But the Tortoise had two friends, a pair of young Geese, who used to fly about near the pond in search of food. And when they heard that things were getting hot for the Tortoise in that pond, because he talked so much, they flew up to him and cried eagerly:

"Oh, Tortoise! do come along with us! We have such a beautiful home away in the mountains, where you may talk all day long, and nobody shall worry you there!"

"All very well," grumbled the Tortoise, "but how am I to get there? I can't fly!"

"Oh, we'll carry you, if you can only keep your mouth shut for a little while."

"Yes, I can do that," says he, "when I like. Let us be off."

So the Geese picked up a stout stick, and one Goose took one end in her bill and the other Goose took the other end, and then they told the Tortoise to get hold in the middle; "only be careful," said they, "not to talk."

The Tortoise set his teeth fast on the stick, and held on like grim death, while the Geese, flapping their strong wings, rose in the air and flew towards their home.

All went well for a time. But it so happened that some boys were looking up in the air, and were highly amused by what they saw.

"Look there!" cried one to the rest, "two Geese carrying a Tortoise on a stick!"

The Tortoise on hearing this was so angry that he forgot all about his danger, and opened his mouth to cry out: "What's that to you? Mind your own business!" But he got no farther than the first word; for when his mouth opened he loosed the stick, down he dropped, and fell with a crash on the stones.

The talkative Tortoise lay dead, with his shell cracked in two.

The Monkeys and the Gardener

Once upon a time there was a beautiful park, full of all manner of trees and shrubs, with beds of flowers set here and there, and no end of fruit-trees. A gardener used to take care of this park; pruning the trees when they made too much wood, and digging the ground, and watering the flowers in dry weather.

It happened that there was a fair to be held away in the city, and the gardener very much wanted to go. But who would take care of the park and garden? If his master came in and found all the flowers drooping or dead, what would he say then! It would never do.

Meditating thus, and in doubt, he looked up into the branches of the trees, and a bright thought struck him. I must tell you that in this park there were not only herds of deer, and plenty of rabbits and other creatures that usually live in parks, but there were troops of monkeys in the trees, who climbed and chattered and cracked nuts all day long, with no lessons to do. And when the gardener cast up his eyes to the trees, he saw some monkeys that he knew very well indeed. Many a time he had been kind to them; and now he thought they should do the like by him, as one good turn deserves another.

So the gardener called out, "Monkeys, I want you!"

Down they all clambered, and in a very short time they were sitting beside him on the grass.

"Monkeys," said he, "I have been a good friend to you, letting you eat my nuts and apples. And now I want to take a holiday. Will you water my garden while I am away?"

"Oh yes, yes, yes!" cried the Monkeys. They thought it a great joke, and leaped for joy.

So the gardener handed over his watering-pots to the monkeys, and put on his Sunday clothes, and went away to the fair.

Meanwhile, the Monkeys held a solemn council, sitting in a ring round the Monkey chief.

"Brothers," said the Monkey chief, "our good friend, the gardener has given us charge of this garden and all there is in it. We must take care not to hurt anything, and, above all, not to waste the water. There is very little water, and I really don't think it will go round."

It was in fact a well, very small at the top, but very deep, and at the bottom the water was always running. You might have watered till doomsday out of that well; but monkeys, though they are cunning, are not wise, and these monkeys thought that a little round hole could not hold very much water.

"So you see," the Monkey chief went on, "you must give each plant just enough water, and no more; and I think the best way will be, to see how long the roots are."

So each Monkey took a watering-pot, and they scattered all over the garden. Every bush and every plant they carefully pulled up, and measured its roots; and then they gave a great deal of water to plants with long roots, and only a little when the roots were short. After that they put the plants and bushes back in the holes they came from.

After a day or two, back came the gardener from his fair. But what was his horror to see that nearly all the plants in the garden were drooping, some of them dead and many dying, while the Monkeys were busy in every direction pulling up the rest.

"Oh dear, oh dear, what in the world are you doing? My garden is ruined, my garden is ruined!" The poor gardener wept for sorrow.

The Chief Monkey was very much surprised. He thought he had been very clever to put water according to the size of the roots, and he said so.

"Clever!" said the gardener. "Clever indeed! Fools you are, there is no mistake about it."

"Fools they may be," said his master, who had come up behind him without being seen, "but, after all, that is their nature. You ought to have known better than to put monkeys in charge of a garden, and you are a greater fool than they."

Then he sent that gardener away and got another.

The Goblin and the Sneeze

Once upon a time there was a very powerful Goblin, who haunted a little house just outside the gates of a city. Nobody else lived in this house. There was a big black beam that ran across from one side to the other, up in the roof; and there this Goblin perched. For twelve years he had served the King of the Goblins faithfully, and as a reward he was now permitted to gobble up any man who sneezed inside that house; and, indeed, that is why these creatures are called Goblins. But if, when a man sneezed, some one else said, "God bless you!" as people do say, or "May you live a hundred years!" then the man who said it was free; and if the other answered, "The same to you!" he was free too. Everybody but these the Goblin might gobble up for a single sneeze.

Now it fell out that one day a father and son were travelling along the road, and they came to the city gates just as the sun went down. I must tell you that in those days the people used to shut the city gates fast at sunset, and nothing would make them open again till the morning—they were horribly afraid of robbers or wild soldiers, who might come and damage them in the night. So when these two wayfarers came up to the gates, and wanted to go in, the porter said no.

"Now, do we look like robbers?" asked the father. Certainly they did not, dusty and grimy with their trudge, and a bag of tools over the shoulder.

"Robbers or no robbers, orders are orders," said the porter, "and this gate doesn't open for the King himself."

"Well, what are we to do?" The poor fellow was in despair.

"Oh, there's an empty house outside; there it is among the trees. It is haunted, they say; but I daresay the Goblin won't hurt you."

"Goblin!—well, we must take our chance, I suppose." Indeed, there was nothing for it; so to the house they went. They rested, and cooked a meal for themselves on a fire of sticks, and then prepared to go to sleep.

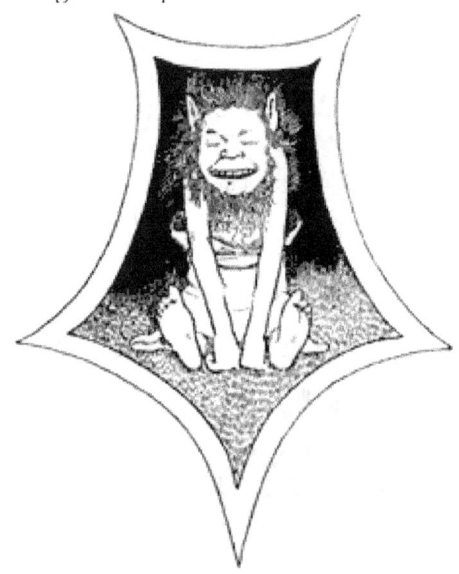

The Goblin, however, was not going to let them off so easily; he wanted his dinner too. After waiting a long time, with never a sneeze from one or the other, he raised a cloud of fine dust; that was rather mean of him, but still he was very hungry, and did not stick at trifles. Sure enough, the father nearly sneezed his head off.

The Goblin chuckled, and made ready to pounce from his perch and devour the pair of them. But the son happened to see him, and, being a sharp lad, he guessed the truth. "God bless you, father!" says he; "may you live a hundred years!"

How the Goblin gnashed his teeth! However, if his pudding was lost, his meat was left; so he stretched out a great claw to clutch the father and tear him to pieces.

Just then the father cried, "Thank you, my son, and the same to you!"

He was only just in time; the claw was within an inch of his throat; but the Goblin, baffled, flew up to his perch again, and sat mouthing and mumbling there.

Then the son began to talk to this Goblin, and showed him the error of his ways, and how cruel he was to eat men; and the end of it was, he persuaded the Goblin to become a vegetarian, and to follow him about, and be his errand-boy. You will think this was a very soft-hearted Goblin. Perhaps no one had ever spoken kindly to him before; anyhow, whatever the reason was, he went out with the two travellers, as tame as a tabby cat; and for all I know, they may be travelling together to this very day.

The Grateful Beasts and the Ungrateful Prince

Once upon a time there was a King, and he had a son. And this son was so cruel and disagreeable, that he took a delight in hurting people, and never spoke to anybody without an oath or a blow. He was a thorn in the flesh to everybody he came across; he was like grit in the porridge, like a fly in the eye, like a stone in the shoon. And they called him the Wicked Prince.

One day the Wicked Prince went down to the river to bathe, along with a number of servants. By-and-by a great storm came on, and the clouds were so thick that it became pitch-dark. However, this Prince was obstinate, and would not give up his bathe; and as he was too lazy even to bathe himself, he swore at his servants, and said:

"You lazy beasts! Bathe me, and look sharp about it, or I'll tickle you with a cat-o'-nine-tails!"

Now the servants had had enough of this young bully; and thought they, "What if we pitch him into the river, where the current is strong, and just leave him there! We can easily pretend he was carried away where we could not reach him; and if the King finds us out, and puts us to death—anyhow, death is better than his eternal bullying." So they pitched him head over heels into the water, though he screamed and struggled, and then they went home and told the King that he had gone in to bathe, and a flood carried him away. I daresay it was wicked of them to tell such a lie, but it was more the Prince's fault than theirs.

Meanwhile the Prince had got hold of a tree that had been torn up by the roots, and climbing upon it, went floating down the river.

Now on the banks of this river lived a Snake. This Snake had once been a very rich man, and he had buried a vast treasure on the river bank; and he loved his riches more than he loved his own soul, so when he died, he was born again as a Snake, and had to live for ever close to his buried hoard. And a Rat that lived

close by had also been a man once, and buried his money as the Snake had done, instead of using it in doing good; so he was born as a Rat, and made a hole where his money lay. These two creatures were caught by the flood, and it so happened that they saw the tree where the Wicked Prince was, and swimming to it, each got on one end, while the Prince was in the middle. And a young Parrot flying through the air, was beaten down by the rain; for in that country the drops of rain are as big as pigeons' eggs, and no birds can fly through it. Then it so happened that this Parrot dropped down upon the same tree where the Snake was, and the Rat, and the Wicked Prince; and so there were four of them on the tree, floating down the river.

As the tree came near to a bend in the river, it was washed close to the bank. And on the bank a man was sitting. He did not mind the rain a bit, because he was a Hermit, who thought the world so wicked that he left it and went to live in the jungle all by himself. He built himself a little hut by the riverside, and, wet or fine, he cared not a jot. This man saw the tree, and managed to catch hold of it and pull it ashore. Then he got the four creatures off it, and took them into his hut, and dried them and warmed them by the fire. But he began with the Parrot, because she looked the most miserable of them all; and then he dried the Rat; and next the Snake; and only attended to the man when he had comforted the other three. This made the Wicked Prince very angry. If he abused even those who made much of him, you may imagine how he cursed and swore in his heart at this man who left him to the last! But he said nothing, because he was afraid that if he did the man might turn him out in the storm again.

In a day or two the rain stopped, and the flood went down; and the creatures were all right again as they took their leave of the Hermit. The Snake thanked him for his kindness and said:

"You have saved my life, good Hermit! What can I do for you? You seem to be a poor man; I am rich, and if you ever want money just come to my hole and call 'Snake,' and you shall have all my treasure. Good-bye!" The Rat said the same.

The Parrot was very sorry to think that she had no money, so she said: "Silver and gold have I none; but if you ever are hungry, and want some rice, come to my tree and call 'Parrot,' and I'll get you as much rice as ever you like."

But the Wicked Prince hated this kind Hermit, because he had been left to the last. However, he pretended to be grateful, and said to the Hermit: "I hope you will pay me a visit soon. I am a Prince, and I shall be glad of a chance to repay you for all you have done for me." Then he went away, chuckling to think how he would torment the poor Hermit, if ever he got him into his power.

This Hermit had all his wits about him, and he knew that people often promise what they never mean to do; so after a while he thought he would put them all to the test. So first he took his stick, and journeyed to the city where the Wicked Prince lived. The Prince, who was King himself now, saw him coming, and thought to himself: "Aha! here's that rascal that left me to the last. Wants me to pay him for it, I suppose! Well, I'll pay him! I'll pay him out!" So he called to his men: "Hi there, brutes! do you see that fellow? He tried to rob me the other day—just catch him and give him a flogging, and then stick a stake through his body, and leave him to die!"

Then the servants caught the Hermit, and flogged him well. But the Hermit did not cry out or grumble, only kept on saying to himself quietly: "The proverb's true, the proverb's true!"

"What proverb do you mean?" they asked him.

"It's unlucky to save a drowning man," said the Hermit.

Then he told them the whole story, and very angry they were when they heard it. They stopped beating the Hermit at once, and seizing the Wicked King, they beat him instead, and stuck a stake through his body, and left him to die.

Then they made the Hermit King instead of the Wicked Prince. And the Hermit took them a walk into the country, and when they came to the Snake's hole he called out "Snake!" Out came the Snake, and curled up against his feet, and showed him the hole where his treasure was; and the Hermit gave it all to his servants. And then they went to the Rat's hole, and he called out "Rat!" And the Rat ran up, and rubbed his nose against the King's hand, and gave him all his treasure, which the King gave to his servants as well as the other. And last of all they went to the Parrot's tree, and called "Parrot!" And the Parrot flew up and gave a call, and instantly all the air was black with Parrots. And all the Parrots carried a grain of rice in their beaks, and dropped it on the ground; and there was such a heap of rice, that it was enough to feed all the people for the rest of their lives.

So the grateful beasts kept their promise, and the ungrateful Prince was killed, and the Hermit ruled over his people kindly, and they all lived happily until they died. And when they died they all went to heaven; and the Snake and the Rat and the Parrot went there too, because they had at last overcome their love of money, and given it away to show how grateful they were to the Hermit for being kind to them.

The Goblin in the Pool

Animals in the forest have no bottles and glasses to drink out of, so if they are thirsty they have to go down to a pool. Now in a certain great forest there was a pool, in which lived a horrible Goblin. He was big and black, like an immense monkey, with an immense mouth, and four rows of sharp teeth; but he could not come out of the water, because he had no nose, but only gills like a fish. So if any animal came down into the water to get a drink, he pounced upon him at once and gobbled him up; but he could not touch the animals while they remained on the bank.

One year there was a great drought, and the sun was so hot that it dried up all the water in that forest for many miles round, except the pool where this Goblin was; but this pool was very deep and cool, under the trees, and therefore it was not dried up. There was a herd of monkeys who had been wandering about for a long time in search of water, but found none, until they came to this pool. But the King of the Monkeys was very clever, and he noticed that there were a great many footprints going down to the water, and none coming away. So he warned his Monkeys not to go near that pool. However, one of them was very thirsty, and ran down into the water; but as soon as he got into the water, and was having a delicious drink—suddenly he disappeared! There were some bubbles, and no more was seen of the Monkey. The other Monkeys watched for a long time, wondering what had become of their friend; and then another, who was so thirsty that he could not help it, stepped quietly into the water and began to drink. In an instant he gave a shriek and threw up his hands, and the others saw him dragged down below the water! A few bubbles came up to the top and burst, but the poor Monkey was gone.

What were they to do? They were dying of thirst, and yet they were afraid to drink; the banks were high, and they could not reach the water from the top. So they all sat round the banks, looking at the water, very unhappy.

By-and-by a man came down to the side of the pool. He wanted a drink of water, but he had no glass. So he looked round, and then he saw the Monkeys sitting on the bank, very unhappy.

"What's the matter?" said he.

"Don't go into that pool!" said the King of the Monkeys. "If you do, you will be drowned, like our two poor friends!"

Then they told him how their friends had gone into the water to drink, and how they had both been pulled underneath and drowned, none of them could tell how.

The man understood at once that it was a Goblin. So he pulled up a long reed that was growing on the bank of the pool and cut off the ends, and then he put down one end of it into the water and sucked at the other end, and the water came up from the pool into his mouth. At this the Monkeys were delighted, and they all pulled up reeds from the bank (for you know a monkey always imitates what he sees men do), and sucked up the water through them, and so quenched their thirst without going into the pool. And the Goblin, finding that no more food was to be got, died of starvation; and a good thing too.

The Foolish Farmer and the King

Once there was a foolish Farmer, who had a son at court, serving the King. This Farmer was a very poor man, and all he had to plough his fields with was one pair of oxen. Two oxen was all he had, and one of them died.

The poor Farmer was in despair. One ox was not enough to draw the plough over the heavy land; and he had no money to buy another. So he sent a message to his son, that he was wanted at home.

When the son came, his father told him that one of his oxen was dead, and he had no money to buy another. So he begged his son to ask the King to give him an ox.

"No, no," said his son, "I am always asking the King for something. If you want an ox, you must ask him yourself."

"I can't do it!" said the poor Farmer. "You know what a muddle-head I am. If I go to ask the King for another ox, I shall end by giving him this one!"

"Well, what must be, must be," said his son. "Anyhow, I cannot ask the King: but I'll train you to do it."

So he led his father to a place which was dotted all over with clumps of grass. The young courtier tied up a number of bundles of this grass, and arranged them in rows. "Now, look here, father," said he, "this is the King, that is the Prime Minister, that is the General, here are the other grandees," pointing to each bundle as he said the name. "When you come into the King's presence, you must begin by saying: 'Long live the King!' and then ask your boon." To help him to remember, the son made up a little verse for his father to say, and this is the verse:

"I had two oxen to my plough, with which my work was done.

Now one is dead: O, mighty king, please give me another one!"

"Well," said the Farmer, "I think I can say that." And he repeated it over and over, bowing and scraping to the bunch of grass that he called the King.

Every day for a whole year the Farmer practised; and how the ploughing got on meanwhile I do not know. Perhaps he lived on the seed-corn, and did not plough at all.

At the end of the year he said to his son:

"Now I know that little verse of yours! Now I can say it before any man! Take me to the King!"

So together father and son trudged away to the King's palace. There on a throne he sat, in gorgeous robes, with his courtiers all around him, the Prime Minister, the General, and all, just as the young man had told his father. But the poor Farmer! his head was beginning to swim already.

"Who is this?" said the King to the Farmer's son, who, as you know, was a courtier, so the King knew him.

"It is my father, Sire," he answered.

"What does he want?" the King asked.

All eyes were turned on the Farmer, who by this time was as red as a turkey-cock, and hardly knew whether he stood on head or heels. However, he plucked up courage, and out came the verse, as pat as a pancake:

"I had two oxen to my plough, with which my work was done.

Now one is dead: O, mighty king, please take the other one!"

The King couldn't help laughing; and he saw there must be a mistake somewhere. "Plenty of oxen at home, eh!" said he, keeping up the joke.

"If so, Sire," said the Farmer's son with a bow, "you must have given them."

The King thought that rather neat. "If I have not given you any so far," said he, smiling, "I will do it now."

And when the pair got home, the Farmer in despair at his blunder, lo and behold in his cowhouse were half a dozen of the finest oxen he had ever seen! So the poor old Farmer got his oxen, though he did make a muddle of the verse.

The Pious Wolf

Once there was a flood, and there was a large rock with a Wolf sleeping on the top. The water came pouring around the rock, and when the Wolf awoke he found himself imprisoned, with no way of getting off, and nothing to eat.

"H'm!" said he to himself, "here I am, caught fast sure enough, and here I shall have to stay yet awhile. Nothing to eat, either! Well," he thought, after a pause, "it is Friday to-day, when people say you ought to fast. Suppose I keep a holy fast to-day? A capital idea!" So he crossed his paws, and pretended to pray, and thought himself very good and pious to be fasting.

A fairy saw this, and heard what he said; and she thought she would just see how much was real and how much was sham. So she changed herself into the shape of a pretty little Kid, and jumped down out of the air on to the rock.

The Wolf opened an eye to see what the noise could be, and there was a tender little Kid, standing on the rock. He forgot his prayers in a minute. "Aha!" said he. "A Kid! I can keep my Friday fast to-morrow. Now for the Kid!" He smacked his lips, and jumped at the Kid.

But the Kid jumped away, and, try as he would, he could not come near it. You know it was the fairy, and the fairy did not let herself be caught.

After trying to catch the Kid for some time the Wolf lay down again. "After all," said he, "it is Friday; and perhaps I had best keep my fast to-day."

"You humbug!" said the fairy, who had gone back to her proper shape; "you are a nice creature to pretend that you are keeping fast! You fast because you can't help it, not because you are really good. As a punishment, you shall stay on this rock till next Friday, and fast for a week!"

So saying, she opened her wings and flew far away.

Birds of a Feather

Once upon a time there was a big horse called Chestnut. He was as fierce as a fury, and bit everybody who came near him; his groom always had a broken bone, or a bruise at the least; and, as for the other horses, let Chestnut loose in the herd, and there was a fine to-do: a kick for one, a bite for another; it was hurry, skurry, worry, till they took themselves off and left him alone in the clover.

Now the King wanted to buy some horses, and a dealer had driven down a couple of hundred of them for the King to buy. But the King was a skinflint, and wanted to get them cheap; so he dropped a hint to his groom, that it would not be a bad thing if Chestnut made acquaintance with these horses; at the same time, he dropped a gold piece in the groom's hand. So the groom led Chestnut by this new herd, and, all of a sudden, he quietly flicked Chestnut with his whip; Chestnut reared and plunged, the groom shouted, and, pretending to find the horse too strong for him, let go the halter. Off galloped Chestnut, kicking up his heels in the air, roaring and whinnying; and fine fun he had among the new horses! By the time he had done with them, hardly one had a whole skin.

The poor dealer was in despair. He would be ruined! And next day, when the King came to see the horses, he turned up his nose. "Pooh! do you suppose I want bruised old hacks like that? Look at that sore! And here is a broken jaw! Why, half of them limp!" In vain the dealer protested that it was Chestnut's fault; the King only laughed, and asked if he expected him to believe that one horse could do all that mischief. (And yet, as you know, it was one horse, and at the King's own bidding too.) However, it was a pity that he should have to take them back again, the King said; so, if he liked, as a favour, he would buy the horses, at half price.

The dealer was not taken in by this, but he pretended to be very grateful, and went home again, wondering what he could do.

He was afraid to offend the King, and, indeed, very few people were rich enough to buy his splendid horses. So he knew that he would be obliged to take some more down to the King another time. Then he suddenly remembered he had just such another vicious brute at home, named Strongjaw, that nobody could do anything with. "Aha!" said he; "I have it! I'll take Strongjaw down with me next time, and if he does not prove a match for Chestnut I am very much mistaken." He chuckled with glee as he thought what a fine fight there would be between the two.

Next time, as he had resolved, he brought Strongjaw with the drove, and as soon as the King's groom came by with Chestnut, and let him go as he did before, the dealer's eyes twinkled, and he let out Strongjaw. Chestnut pricked up his ears, and Strongjaw pricked up his; then, without taking any notice of the rest, they trotted up to each other and rubbed noses, and began to lick each other all over. They did not fight at all, but in a moment they became bosom friends.

The dealer could not understand this, neither could the King. However, this time the King had to pay a good price for the horses, and as he saw his little trick was found out, he felt rather ashamed of himself, and so he paid the man for the other horses as well. Still, they kept wondering and wondering what the reason could be that these two horses, each so fierce and wild, were quiet as a pair of kittens together. The King asked the wisest man in all his kingdom to explain it; and the man, who was a minstrel, that is, he used to sing songs to the King about all that had happened or would happen in the world, took up his harp and sang:

"If the reason you would know,
Like to like will always go;
Here's a pair of vicious horses
Just the same in all their courses;
Both are wild, and bite their tether:
Birds of a feather flock together."

Spend a Pound to Win a Penny

Some people were steaming peas under a tree, in order to make a meal for their horses. Up in the branches sat a Monkey, who watched with his restless eyes what they were doing.

"Aha!" thought the Monkey. "I spy my dinner!"

So when they had finished steaming the peas, and turned away for a moment to look after the horses, gently, gently, the Monkey let himself down from the tree. He grabbed at the peas, and stuffed his mouth with them, and both hands as full as they could hold, then he clambered up to his perch as best he could. There he sat, his wizened old face happy and cunning, eating the peas.

Suddenly one pea fell.

"O dear, O dear! O my pea, my pea!" cried the Monkey, gibbering in distress. The other peas began to fall out of his mouth, but he did not notice them. He wrung his hands in despair, and the peas began to fall out of his hands too, but he took no notice. All he thought of was this, that one pea was gone.

So he shinned down the trunk, and scrambled about on the ground, hunting for his lost pea, but he could not find it anywhere.

By this time the men had come back, after seeing to their horses. When they saw a monkey meddling with their cooking-pots they all waved their arms, and called out, "Shoo! shoo!" Then they picked up stones, and began to pelt the Monkey with them. This terrified the Monkey so much that he gave one jump to the nearest branch, and swung himself up to the top of the tree.

"After all," said he to himself, "it was only one pea." But he ought to have thought of that before, for now like a thunderclap, it came home to him, that somehow or other all the other peas had gone too.

That day the Monkey had to content himself with the smell of boiled peas for dinner, and I hope the loss taught him not to be so greedy in future.

The Cunning Crane and the Crab

Once upon a time a number of fish lived in a little pool. It was all very well while there was rain; but when summer came, and it began to be very hot, the water dried up and got lower and lower, until there was hardly enough to hide the fish.

Now not far away there was a beautiful lake, always fresh and cool; for it lay under the shadow of great trees, and it was covered all over with water-lilies. And a Crane lived on the banks of this lake.

The Crane used to eat fish, when he could catch any; and one day, coming to the little pool, he saw all the fish gasping in it, and thought of a neat trick to get hold of them without trouble.

"Dear Fish," said the Crane, "I am so sorry to see you cooped up in this hole. I know a beautiful lake close by, deep and fresh and cool, and if you like I will carry you there."

The Fish did not know what to make of this, because never since the world began had a crane done a good turn to a fish. You see it is just as absurd to suppose that a crane would help fish, as to think that a cat would be kind to a mouse.

So they said to the Crane, "We don't believe you; what you want is to eat us."

This was just what the Crane did want, but he did not say so. "No, no!" said he; "I'm not so cruel as all that. I have eaten a fish now and then"—he saw it was of no use denying that, because they knew he had—"but I have plenty of other food, and it goes to my heart to see you here. In this hot water you will all be boiled fish before long!"

"That's true enough," said the Fish; "the water is hot." Well, the end of it was, they persuaded an old Fish with one eye to go and see.

The Crane took the one-eyed Fish in his beak and put him in the lake; and when he had seen that what the Crane said was true so far, he carried the Fish back again to tell the others.

The old Fish could not say enough to praise the lake. "It's ever so big," he said, "and deep and cool, just as the Crane said; and there are trees overshadowing it, and water-lilies are growing in the mud; and the whole of it is covered with fine fat flies! Ah, what a feast I have had!" And he rolled up his one eye at the thought of it.

Then all the Fish were eager to go. And now it was who should be first; every Fish was anxious to remain no longer in the pool. They came to the top of the water, all begging the Crane to take them to this beautiful lake.

"One at a time!" said the Crane. "I have only one beak, you know!" And he smiled to himself, for that beak was made to eat fish, not to carry them.

However, it was decided that as the one-eyed Fish had been so brave as to trust himself in the Crane's beak, before he knew what the truth was, he certainly deserved to go first.

So the Crane took the one-eyed Fish in his beak, and carried him over to the lake. But this time he did not drop the Fish in; he laid him in the cleft of a tree, and pecked his one eye out with his beak; then he killed him, and ate him up, and dropped his bones at the foot of the tree.

By-and-by the Crane came back for another. "Now then, who's next?" asked the Crane. "Old One-eye is swimming about, as happy as a king!" He picked up another fish, and served him like the first, dropping his bones at the foot of the tree.

And so it went on, until in a few days the pool was empty. The cunning Crane had eaten every single one of the fish! He stood on the bank, peering into every hole, to see whether there might not be a little one left somewhere. There was one, surely! No, it was a Crab. Never mind, he thought; all's fish that comes to my net!

So he invited the Crab to come with him to the lake.

"Why, how are you going to carry me?" asked the Crab.

"In my beak, to be sure!" replied the Crane.

"You might drop me," said the Crab, "and then I should split."

"Oh no, I promise I won't drop you!" said the Crane. But the Crab had more sense than all the fish put together, and he did not believe in the Crane's friendship at all. So he still pretended to hesitate, and at last he said:

"Well, I'll tell you what. I can hold on tighter with my claws than you can with your beak. I'll come, but you must let me hold on to your neck with my claws. Then I shall feel safe."

The Crane was so hungry that, without stopping to think, he agreed; and then the Crab got tight hold of his neck with his claws, and the Crane carried him towards the lake.

But after a while the Crab saw that he was being carried somewhere else, indeed to that tree where the Crane used to sit and eat the fish.

"Crane dear," said he, "aren't you going to put me in the lake?"

"Crane dear, indeed!" said the Crane, "do you suppose I was born to carry crabs about? Not I! Just look at that heap of bones under yon tree! Those are the bones of the fish that used to live in your pool. I ate them, and I'm going to eat you!"

"Are you, though!" said the Crab, and gave the Crane's neck a little nip.

Then the Crane saw what a fool he had been to let a Crab put a claw round his neck. He knew that the Crab could kill him if he liked, and he was frightened to death at the thought. People who try to deceive others often pay for it themselves; and that is what happened to the Crane.

"Dear Crab!" said he, with tears streaming from his eyes, "forgive me! I won't kill you, only let me go!"

"Just put me in the lake, then," said the Crab.

The Crane stepped down to the lakeside, and laid the Crab upon the mud. And the Crab, as soon as he felt himself safe, nipped off the Crane's head as clean as if it had been cut with a knife.

So perished the treacherous Crane, caught by his own trick. And the Crab lived happily in the beautiful lake for the rest of his life.

Union is Strength

There once was a clever Fowler who used to hunt quails. He could imitate the quail's note exactly; and when he had found a hiding-place, he used to sit hidden in it, and call out the quail's note, until a number of quails had come together; then he threw a net over them, and bagged them all.

But amongst the quails was one very clever bird, and he hit on the following device: He told the quails, when they felt the net drop over them, that each one should pop his head through one of the meshes of the net, and then at the word, away they should fly together.

All fell out as he arranged. Next day the Fowler sounded his imitation of the quail's note, and the birds flocked from far and near; then, when a good many had gathered in a clump within his reach, he cast the net, which fell over them and made them all prisoners. They all did what the wise Quail had told them; each quail put his head through one of the meshes, then at a word they were all away together, bearing the net with them. After some little time they saw a large bush, and dropped upon this bush; then the net was held up by the bush, while all the birds got away underneath.

Again and again this happened, until the Fowler began to despair; he came home every night empty-handed, and besides that he had lost ever so many nets.

Why did he keep on trying to catch them, then? Because he thought that sooner or later they would begin to quarrel, and then the game would be his.

And quarrel they soon did. One Quail happened to tread on another's toe.

"What are you doing, clumsy?" said the second Quail angrily.

"I'm very sorry," said the first; "I really did not mean to tread on your toe."

"You did!"

"I tell you I didn't!"

"What a lie!"

"A lie, is it? Hoity, toity, how high-and-mighty we are, to be sure! I suppose it is you lift up the net, all by yourself, when the man throws it over us!"

And so they went on, getting angrier and angrier. And the result was, that next day, when the fowler made his cast, said the first Quail to the second:

"Now then, Samson, lift away! They say that last time your feathers all fell off your head!"

"Oh, indeed! They say that when you tried to lift, both your wings moulted! Lift away, and let us see if it is true!"

But while they were quarrelling, and each telling the other to lift the net, the Fowler lifted it for them, and crammed them all together into his basket, and took them home for supper.

Silence is Golden

Once upon a time a Lion had a she-jackal for his mate, and they had a young one. This Cub was just like his sire to look at, in shape and colour, mane and claws; but in voice he took after his dam. So you would fancy he was a lion, so long as he held his tongue.

This Cub used to play about with the young Lions, and merry times they had to be sure, tumbling head over heels, and trying to knock each other down. One day, in the midst of their game, the mongrel Cub thought he would frighten them; so he opened his mouth wide, intending to roar, and all that came out was a yelp like the yelp of a jackal. The other young Lions were quite shocked; they could not imagine what strange creature this was. One of them went up to the old Lion, who was watching them, and said:

"Lion's claws and lion's paws
Lion's feet to stand upon;
But the bellow of this fellow
Sounds not like a lion's son!"

"You are right," said the old Lion; "his dam was a Jackal." And then, turning to the poor Cub, who was looking very crestfallen, he said:

"All will see what kind you be
If you yelp as once before;
So don't try it, but keep quiet,
Yours is not a lion's roar."

The poor Cub slunk away with his tail between his legs, while the other Lions sniffed and turned up their noses at him. Ever after that he took good care to hold his tongue when he was in the company of his betters.

The Great Yellow King and His Porter

Once upon a time, in a great and rich city, reigned a mighty King, who was called by the title of the Great Yellow King. This King was very cruel to his people, and ground them like grist in the mill; he robbed them of their goods, many he cast into prison, others he ill-treated, cutting off an arm, or a leg, or blinding them, and some he put to death without cause. He was just as bad at home; when he was a boy he did nothing but tease his sisters, pulling their hair and putting spiders down their necks; and now that he was grown up he made life a misery to wife and child. He was like a speck of dust that gets into your eye, or a thorn in the heel, or grit between your teeth.

But it is a long lane that has no turning; and at last the Great Yellow King died. When a king or queen dies, people are generally very sorry, and wear mourning for them; but when the Great Yellow King died there was such rejoicing and merriment as had not been known for many a long day. All the shops were shut, and all the schools had a whole holiday; there were raree-shows and merry-go-rounds, and everybody high and low was half daft with joy.

But one man was not joyful. On the steps of the palace sat the Yellow King's porter, sighing and sobbing, weeping and wailing. No one could understand it; everybody in the whole town was glad, and here was this porter crying! At last some one asked him why he cried.

"What is the matter?" said he. "Was the Great Yellow King so kind to you as all that? I never heard of his being kind to anybody!"

"No, it isn't that!" sobbed the man.

"Well, what is it then?"

The man looked up and rubbed his eyes. "Well," said he, "I'll tell you. When his majesty used to come out of his palace, down the steps, he always gave me a cuff on the head, and another when he came back. What a fist his majesty had, to be sure! Now if he tries that game on with the porter who sits by the gates of Death, I am very much afraid they won't have him there at any price, and then he will come back to us!"

But the other man laughed, and said, "Don't be afraid of that, Porter! He's dead and done for, and however much they wish it, they can never send him back to us again."

So the Porter was comforted, and wiped his eyes, and went to get a glass of beer.

The Quail
and the Falcon

There once was a young Quail that lived on a farm. When the farmer ploughed up the land, Quailie used to hop about over the clods and pick up seeds, or weeds, or worms, or anything that the plough turned up, and he ate these and lived on them.

You might think this was very nice for him; he had no trouble to find food, because the ploughman turned it up; he had only to hop along after the plough and peck. Not a bit of it; he must needs better himself, as he said; so one fine day he flew away over the farm, away to the forest which fringed it; and, alighting on the ground just where the forest began, he looked about to see if there was anything good to eat.

Up in the air, just above the tree-tops, a Falcon was sailing, poised on outstretched wings; as Quailie searched for worms, so the Falcon was searching for quails; and lo and behold, he spied one! Down he came with a swoop and a whirr, and in an instant the Quail was in his crooked claws.

What could poor Quailie do now? He twittered and fluttered, and at last began to cry.

"Oh dear, oh dear!" whimpered Quailie, the tears running down his beak, "what a fool I was to poach on other people's preserves! If I had only stayed at home this Falcon could never have caught me, not even if he had come and tried!"

"What's that, Quailie?" asked the Falcon. "Do you think I can't catch you anywhere?"

"Not on my own ground!" cried the Quail.

"What do you mean by that?"

"A ploughed field full of clods."

"Oh, nonsense, Quailie, clods won't help you. Just try; off you go! I'll follow."

The Quail flew off, feeling as happy now as he was miserable a moment gone; and when he got back to his farm he picked out a big clod and perched on the top. "Come on, Falcon!" cried he; "come on!"

Down came the Falcon with a swoop like a flash of lightning; but just as he came close the Quail dodged him nimbly and tumbled over the clod to the other side, leaving the Falcon to come full tilt against the clod of earth; and so swift was he, that the shock killed him.

So the Quail found out how much better it is for most people to stick to what they are used to; and as for the Falcon, he might have thought, if he had been able to think at all, that a bird in the hand is worth two in the bush.

Pride Must Have a Fall

Once upon a time there was a beautiful wild Goose that lived in the mountains; he was King of the Geese, and he had a mate and two or three fine young ones. But it had happened once that this Goose, in his travels about the world, fell in with a young lady Crow, who was very pretty; as black as jet, with two eyes like black beads, and she flirted and flouted so enchantingly that he had married her, like the goose he was; so he had two wives, the little black Crow and the Goose.

In course of time this Crow laid a beautiful egg, all white with blue spots, and twice as big as an ordinary crow's egg. She was very proud of her egg, and sat on it for a longtime, until one day, pop! went the egg, and out came a funny little chick. The Crow did not know what to make of this chick; he was not black, as she was, and he was not white, like his father, but something betwixt and between, a dingy grey with brown streaks. So she named him Streaky.

Be sure that Streaky fancied himself mightily, being so very different from all the Crows he lived with; he was larger, to begin with, and then he had a very loud voice, with several different notes in it; not to mention his brown streaks, which made him a proud bird indeed. And I think the other Crows took him at his own price, as foolish creatures are apt to do, and thought him very wonderful, though he was really only a mongrel.

Now the Goose, his father, used to pay a visit to the Crow colony now and again, flying down from the mountains to the dust-heap where they lived, outside the city gate. But he did not stay long, because the Crows used to feed on offal and dead bodies, in fact anything dirty they could find; and King Goose could not get what he liked to eat.

Well, once as he was talking to his sons, the young Geese, they asked him why he was always going away for days at a time.

"Why," said he, "I go to see a son of mine that lives somewhere else."

"Oh, how nice!" said the Geese. "Then he must be our brother. Do let us bring him here on a visit! Do, father!"

At first the father Goose would not let them go, for fear of mischief; but after a while he was persuaded, and gave them very careful directions how to fly, and where to go, and how to find the place where Streaky lived, on the top of a tall palm-tree that grew out of a dust-heap at the city gate.

So away they flew, and away they flew, till at last they saw the tall palm-tree; and on the very top of it, a big nest; and in the nest, a little black Crow, and our funny friend Streaky.

They said "How do you do?" and told their errand; because they meant to go through with it now, although they did not much like the look of this ugly bird Streaky, with his airs and graces. Mrs. Crow was very much pleased, but Streaky looked bored, and said:

"Aw, caw, I don't think I can fly all that way. It is really too much trouble. Why did not the Governor come to see me instead, as usual—aw?" This rude bird called his father the Governor; you see, as he had been brought up among carrion crows, his manners were none of the best.

The young Geese began to like him less than ever. However, they put a good face on it, and answered him:

"Well, Streaky, if you are as weak as all that, we will carry you on a stick."

These Geese were very big, strong birds, and they thought nothing of carrying Streaky. So they looked about until they found a strong stick, and then each of them took an end in his mouth, and Streaky perched in the middle. They could not say good-bye to Mrs. Crow, because their mouths were full of the stick, but they made her a nice bow, like polite little Geese, and flew off.

As for Streaky, he was far too full of his own importance to say good-bye to his mother, or even so much as "Thank you" to the two birds who were so kindly carrying him. There he sat, on the middle of the stick, as proud as Punch, pluming his feathers, and feeling that now all the world would see what a splendid bird he was.

As they flew over the city Streaky looked down, and saw the king of the city, in a beautiful carriage drawn by four white thoroughbreds, driving round the city in great state and grandeur. "Aha!" thought he, "that's as it should be! But I'm every bit as good as he!" and in his joy he began to sing a little song which he made up on the spur of the moment, and here is his song:

"As yonder king goes galloping with his milk-white four-in-hand,

Streaky has these, his pair of Geese, to carry him over the land!"

The Geese were very angry when they heard Streaky sing this song. But they were very well-bred Geese, as you must have seen already; so they said nothing at all to him then, but carried him safely to their home, and then they told their father what Streaky had said, so that he might do as he thought best.

Old King Goose was more angry than they were, and was very sorry he had left his son to be brought up by a Crow who knew no manners. So he called Streaky, and this is what he said:

"Streaky, you have been very rude to your brothers, who are at least as good as you; and if you think they are like a pair of horses, to be driven about for your pleasure, you make a great mistake. So the best thing you can do is to fly back to your mother; for your manners suit the dust-heap better than the mountains."

I don't know whether Streaky was ashamed of what he had said; creatures like Streaky are very thick-skinned, and it takes a great deal to make them ashamed; but anyhow he had to go back, and this time he must fly by himself, for it was hardly likely that his brothers would carry him when he had been so rude. He got back a few days later, tired and hungry, and spent the rest of his days on the dust-heap, eating carrion. What his mother thought of it all I don't know; but King Goose never went to see them any more.

The Bold Beggar

There was once a King who was so fond of good eating and drinking that they called him King Dainty. He often spent as much as a thousand pounds on a single dish; which is great wastefulness, when you can dine heartily for a shilling. He thought that if people could not eat things so nice as his, yet they must greatly enjoy seeing him eat them. So he fitted up a beautiful tent outside his own door, and there he took his meals, sitting on a golden throne, under a white silk umbrella. Anybody who liked could see him eat his dinner without charge. This was very generous, wasn't it?

A man who had often seen him eat thought he would like a taste of the King's choice food. And this is what he did.

He came running towards the crowd who, as usual, were watching the King eat his dinner, and shouted: "News! news! news!" Now at that time there were no newspapers, and no posts, and no telegraphs; so any one who brought news was sure of instant hearing. Accordingly the crowd made way for him at once, and he ran up to the King, looking very much excited, and shouting "News!" Then he fell down before the King, as if he were faint with hunger, and gasped.

"Poor fellow!" said the King. "Give him something to eat."
So they propped him up on a chair, and the King fed him out of
his own dish, and gave him delicious wine to drink. The man
made a hearty meal, I can tell you. They thought he never would
finish; but he did finish at last, after an hour or two.

Then the King said to him: "Now, my good fellow, let us hear your news."

"The news is, your Majesty," said the man, "that an hour ago I was hungry, and now I am not!"

All the people looked shocked at his impertinence. But the King only laughed, and said: "That news is true of most of us every day of our lives. Well, you are a bold fellow; this time you may go free, but I advise you not to try it again."

The man bowed low, and went away happy in the success of his trick. I don't know whether the King spent less money upon his dinner after that, but I am quite sure that no one else got a meal at his table in the same way.

The Jackal Would A-Wooing Go

Once upon a time there was a family of Lions that lived in the Himalaya Mountains in a Golden Cave. They were three brothers and one sister. Near by was a silver mountain with a Crystal Cave, and in this Crystal Cave lived a Jackal.

The young Lions used to be out all day, hunting, while their sister kept everything neat and tidy at home. When they caught anything they used to keep a bit for her, because they were not greedy Lions, and they thought that if she did the work at home she deserved some of the game they got abroad.

Now this Jackal fell violently in love with the young Lioness. She was very beautiful, with soft brown fur, and large soft eyes, and fine whiskers; and he did not stop to think what a mongrel cur a Jackal looks beside a Lion, how small, and sneaking, and snarling; so that it was the height of impertinence even to think of such a thing. He did think of it, and more, he actually proposed to the Lioness! You shall hear how he did it.

He had the sense to wait until the three brothers had gone out hunting for food; and then he came and tapped on the rock at the mouth of the Golden Cave. The Lioness looked out, and very much surprised was the Lioness to see the Jackal there. She knew him by sight, of course, as a neighbour; and, indeed, when he was in his Crystal Cave you could always see him, perched up in the air as it might be; for you can see through crystal like glass, and it looked just as if there were nothing there. But they were not on visiting terms, so the Lioness was surprised to see him come tapping at her door. She gave him a distant bow, and waited.

"Beautiful Lioness!" said he, "I love you! see how much we are alike! You have four feet, and so have I; clearly we are made for one another. Will you marry me? We shall be so happy together!"

This offer so astonished the Lioness that she could say nothing. She hated the vile creature, vilest of all creatures; that he should dare to address himself to a royal lioness! a scavenger to a queen! The very thought of the insult made her furious. She resolved that, after such a thing as that had spoken to her, she might just as well die, either by holding her breath or by starving herself. As these thoughts passed through her mind the Jackal was waiting for his answer; but no answer he got. This seemed a pretty broad hint that he was not wanted there; so he went home again, very woebegone, with his tail between his legs, and lay down in his Crystal Cave in much misery.

By-and-by the eldest brother of the Lioness came home again, with a fine fat deer which he had killed. "Here, sister," he called out, "have a bit!"

She put on a very gloomy air. "No," she said, "I think I shall have to die."

"Why, what on earth is the matter?" asked he.

"A nasty, dirty Jackal came, and wanted to marry me!"

"The brute!" said her brother. "Where is he?"

"Can't you see him, lying up in the sky?" You know the crystal was transparent, and as she had never been there she could not tell he was really in a cave.

Off galloped the young Lion, furious with rage, and when he got near the place where the Jackal was lying in his Crystal Cave, he leaped at him, when—crack! went his skull against the wall of crystal, and down fell the Lion—dead!

Just as the Lioness was getting anxious about her eldest brother, the second came in. She told him the same tale, though she was beginning to be sorry that she was going to die. He had not hurt her, after all; and how nice the meat smelt! But the second Lion did not give her much time to think; he growled, and off he went, leaped into the air, cracked his crown against the wall of crystal, and fell down dead beside his brother.

Now when the third brother came in, the Lioness was quite sure she didn't mean to die. However, she looked as gloomy as ever, and told her brother what had happened; he had better go out and see what was become of the other two. Surely two Lions were a match for any Jackal! Still, there he was, as before, up in the air.

"Up in the air?" said the youngest brother, who was cleverer than all the rest put together. "Stuff and nonsense! Now let me think. There must be something for him to lie upon; and yet you can see through it." He scratched his head with one paw and looked wise. "I have it! Crystal, of course, or glass—that's what it is!" So up he jumped, and when he got near the Crystal Cave, there were his two brothers, dead, with their skulls cracked right across like a teacup.

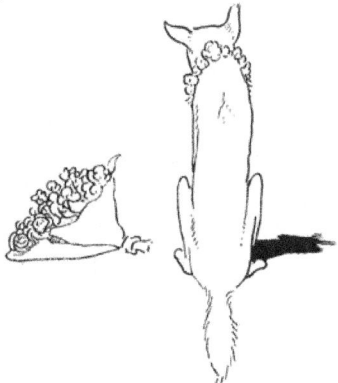

He sat down again, and scratched his head with the other paw. "H'm! it looks as though it may be difficult to get at this

Jackal. However, I'll try kindness first. Jackie, Jackie dear!" he called out.

Now you must know that Lions have a very loud voice, and, if you have heard them talking in the Zoo, you will know that even when they want to coax and purr they are enough to frighten you. And so the poor Jackal, who, after all, was not so bad as the proud Lioness made out, when he heard the Lion coaxing him down, thought "What an awful roar!" His heart was beating very hard before, but this time it gave such a leap that something went snap! And the Jackal was dead too.

Then the Lion looked up, and saw that the Jackal was dead. So he buried his brothers, and went and told his sister all about it. You might expect her to be sorry that her two brave brothers were dead, all because she held her nose so high in the air; but not a bit of it; she was quite satisfied so long as one was left to catch food for her. So she lived all the rest of her life in the Golden Cave, but I never heard that any other animal asked her to marry him.

The Lion and the Boar

Once upon a time there was a Lion who lived in the mountains, and he used to drink water out of a beautiful lake. It so happened that, as he was drinking there one day, he saw a Boar feeding over on the opposite bank. Now he had just eaten a leg of elephant, and was not hungry; but he made a note of that Boar, thinking to himself what a nice meal the Boar would make some other day. So, after drinking his fill, he crawled quietly away through the bushes, hoping that the Boar could not see him. But the Boar had sharp eyes, and did see him. "Hullo!" said he to himself, "yon Lion is afraid of me, that's clear! Ah well, he need not think to get off so easy. If he wants to go, he must fight me first!" He puffed his chest out very big, and rubbed his tusks against a tree, then he called out:

"Stay, stay, runaway!
Let us have a fight to-day!
You have four feet, so have I!
If you fail, you can but try!"

The Lion could hardly believe his ears. What! a Boar challenge him to fight! He could break a Boar's back with a tap of his paw. Still, he hid his astonishment at this impertinent Boar and only said:

"Please, Mr. Boar, let me off to-day, as I'm rather tired; I have just been wrestling with a fox. But, if you like, I will meet you here this day week, and then we can fight it out between us."

He said this so humbly that the Boar became haughtier than ever. "Oh, very well," said he, "it shall never be said I took a mean advantage of any one. This day week, then! Good-day to you."

When he got home, his friends hardly knew him. Every bristle on his back was standing up straight; his little greedy eyes were gleaming; he ran into the house, knocking over the pots and pans, snarling at his wife, and making himself very disagreeable indeed. At last the other Boars protested, and said they would not stand it any longer. "Oho!" says he, "you defy a Boar that has killed a Lion! Come on, then!" and very fierce indeed he looked.

Killed a Lion! They did open their eyes. "Where is the Lion you have killed?" asked a pretty little sow, full of curiosity.

"Well, I haven't exactly killed him yet," said the Boar rather unwillingly. "He is coming to be killed this day week."

"What on earth do you mean?" his friends asked. He told them the story, but he did not feel quite so bold now as he had felt before. And when he finished, he felt worse than ever; for one and all they set up such a weeping and wailing that the whole forest resounded with it! "Oh dear, oh dear!" they cried, "you'll be the death of us! Kill a Lion? Why, he will crunch you up in a trice, and then he'll come here, and we are all dead Boars!"

By this time the poor Boar had lost all his conceit; you see he was an ignorant Boar, and did not know at all what the strength of a Lion is. So his heart was down in his toes, and all he wanted now was some way out of the mischief. Nobody could think of a way, until one very old and wise Boar advised him to roll in the mud till he was very dirty, because Lions are clean beasts and do not like dirt.

So every day he rolled and wallowed in the dirtiest places he could find; and by the appointed time he was like a big cake of dirt. So when he came to the lake where he was to meet the Lion, the wind took a whiff of him to the Lion, and the Lion gave a jump, and snuffed, and sneezed, and swished his tail, and cried out, "Get to leeward, get to leeward! Here's a pretty trick! Well, you have saved your life; I would not touch you with a pair of tongs now!" and, in great disgust he went away, saying, as he went, this little rhyme:

"Dirty Boar, I want no more,
You're saved from being eaten;
If you would fight, I yield me quite,
And own that I am beaten!"

You may be sure that our friend the Boar did not wait any longer, but scampered off home. But when he got there, I am sorry to say he told all his friends he had beaten the Lion, and the Lion had run away! He certainly had beaten the Lion in one way, but not in fair fight, so it was rather mean to pretend he had. However, nobody believed him, and the colony of Boars thought the best thing they could do was to get away from that place as fast as their four legs could carry them. "If he is beaten," said they with a wink, "still, after all, he is a Lion."

The Goblin City

Long, long ago, in the island of Ceylon, there was a large city full of nothing but Goblins. They were all She-goblins, too; and if they wanted husbands, they used to get hold of travellers and force them to marry; and afterwards, when they were tired of their husbands, they gobbled them up.

One day a ship was wrecked upon the coast near the goblin city, and five hundred sailors were cast ashore. The She-goblins came down to the seashore, and brought food and dry clothes for the sailors, and invited them to come into the city. There was nobody else there at all; but for fear that the sailors should be frightened away, the Goblins, by their magic power, made shapes of people appear all around, so that there seemed to be men ploughing in the fields, or shepherds tending their sheep, and huntsmen with hounds, and all the sights of the quiet country life. So, when the sailors looked round, and saw everything as usual, they felt quite secure; although, as you know, it was all a sham.

The end of it was, that they persuaded the sailors to marry them, telling them that their own husbands had gone to sea in a ship, and had been gone these three years, so that they must be drowned and lost for ever. But really, as you know, they had served others in just the same way, and their last batch of husbands were then in prison, waiting to be eaten.

In the middle of the night, when the men were all asleep, the She-goblins rose up, put on their hats, and hurried down to the prison; there they killed a few men, and gnawed their flesh, and ate them up; and after this orgie they went home again. It so happened that the captain of the sailors woke up before his wife came home, and not seeing her there, he watched. By-and-by in she came; he pretended to be asleep, and looked out of the tail of his eye. She was still munching and crunching, and as she munched she muttered:

"Man's meat, man's meat,
That's what Goblins like to eat!"

She said it over and over again, then lay down; and soon she was snoring loudly.

The captain was horribly frightened to find he had married a Goblin. What was he to do? They could not fight with Goblins, and they were in the Goblins' power. If they had a ship they might have sailed away, because Goblins hate the water worse than a cat; but their ship was gone. He could think of nothing.

However, next morning, he found a chance of telling his mates what he had discovered. Some of them believed him, and some said he must have been dreaming; they were sure their wives would not do such a thing. Those who believed him agreed that they would look out for a chance of escape.

But there was a kind fairy who hated those Goblins; and she determined to save the men. So she told her flying horse to go and carry them away. And accordingly, as the men were out for a walk next day, the captain saw in the air a beautiful horse with large white and gold wings. The horse fluttered down, and hovered just above them, crying out, in a human voice:

"Who wants to go home? who wants to go home? who wants to go home?"

"I do, I do!" called out the sailors.

"Climb up, then!" said the horse, dropping within reach. So one climbed up, and then another, and another; and, although the horse looked no bigger than any other horse, there was room for everybody on his back. I think that somehow, when they got up, the fairy made them shrink small, till they were no bigger than so many ants, and thus there was plenty of room for all. When all who wanted to go had got up on his back, away flew the beautiful horse and took them safely home.

As for those who remained behind, that very night the Goblins set upon them and mangled them, and munched them to mincemeat.

Lacknose

There was once a Gardener who had no nose, and he had a very nice garden full of beautiful flowers: roses, and pinks, and lilies, and violets, and all the prettiest flowers you can imagine.

Three little boys thought they would like a bunch of flowers, but they did not know how to get it. So one of them went into the garden and said:

"Good morning, Mr. Lacknose!"

"Good morning, boy," said the Gardener.

The boy thought the best thing he could do was to flatter the old fellow, so he had made up a verse of poetry that he thought very pretty, and so he said to the Gardener:

"Cut, and cut, and cut again,

Hair and whiskers grow amain:

And your nose will grow like these:

Give me a little posy, please!"

The Gardener knew very well that his nose would not grow again like his whiskers, and he thought the little boy rather rude to mention it; so he became angry.

"Go away!" said he, "and get your posy somewhere else!"

The boy went away disappointed; but the second boy thought he would try his luck too. Perhaps the first boy had not spoken nicely; and he had made a verse of poetry too, which he thought would just suit the old Gardener. So in he came with "Good morning, Mr. Lacknose!"

"Good morning, boy," said the old man. "And what do *you* want?"

Then the boy put on a coaxing smile, and said:

"In the autumn seeds are sown,

And ere long they're fully grown;

May your nose sprout up like these!

Give me a little posy, please!"

"There!" he thought, "the old fellow will like that, because he is a Gardener." But not a bit of it! The Gardener saw through his trick, and was angrier than ever.

"Be off!" said he, "or I'll be after you with a stick! Plant a nose, indeed! You had better go somewhere and learn manners before you ask for my flowers!"

So the second boy went away faster than the first.

But the third boy was an honest little boy, and knew that there is nothing like the truth; so he determined to try what truth could do. He walked modestly into the garden and said:

"Good morning, sir!"

"What, another of 'em!" growled the Gardener to himself. "Another pack of lies, I suppose!" He would hardly look at the boy. But the boy, nothing daunted, repeated his verse:

"Babbling fools! to think that they
Can get a posy in this way!
Say they yes, or say they no,
Noses cut no more will grow.
See, I ask you honestly:
Give a posy, sir, to me!"

The Gardener was so pleased to find a straightforward and honest little boy, that he took his scissors and cut a most beautiful bunch of flowers, which he gave the boy with a smile. The boy said, "Thank you, sir, very much!" and went away delighted.

The King's Lesson

Once upon a time there lived a very good King, whose name was Godfrey. Of course, when a man is King, everybody is ready to call him good; but this King really was good. He used to hold courts of justice for people to come to when they had a quarrel; and he decided all the cases so wisely that nobody durst bring an unjust cause before him. So after a while the result was, that the courts became empty; all the rustle and bustle was quiet, the wigs and gowns were hung up on pegs, and as dusty as dusty could be; and nobody had any quarrels at all.

"What a blessing!" thought King Godfrey to himself. "Now we have a little peace. And they say it's all my doing! I wonder if I am really as good as people make me out. Suppose I try to see?" No sooner said than done with this King. He asked one and he asked another; he begged and prayed them to tell him of his faults, so that he might mend them; but no, they said they really could not tell him of his faults, when he had none to tell of. He tried in the palace, he tried in the city; high and low, to and fro, it was just the same: all praise and no blame.

THE KING'S LESSON.

"Well, upon my word," thought the King, "I had no idea I was such a good fellow. Still, who knows what they say behind my back? Happy thought! I'll disguise myself, and that will soon show me the truth." So he dressed himself like a traveller, and got a carriage and pair, and drove all over the country, asking everybody what they thought of the King. Wonder of wonders! they said the same behind his back as they did to his face! That must have been a very nice country to live in, but I am sure I cannot tell where it is.

Now in such a strange country as that, strange things will happen; and so it turned out that, as our King was driving along, he came to a narrow lane sunk between two steep banks, with only just room for the carriage; and right in the middle of this lane another carriage met him. There they stood, both of them, and neither would budge. Our King did not know who was in that carriage, but I will tell you who it was. This was the King of the next country, who was also a good king as kings go, though not so good as the first; and he had got the same idea into his head, that he would wander about in disguise, and find out what people thought of him. Everybody had a good word for him too, it seems; but if he found no one to pick faults in him before, here was one now, as you shall see.

"Get out of the way!" said the driver of the other carriage.

"Get out of the way yourself!" said King Godfrey's man. "I have a King inside," said he; you see, he knew who the disguised traveller was, and he thought there was no need to hide it now, when it might save him trouble.

"If you have one King, I have another!" said the other man; and imagine how astonished King Godfrey's coachman was to hear that.

"Oh dear, oh dear," he said, "what is to be done? Both Kings! How old is your King?" he added suddenly, hoping, you see, that the younger might be willing to give way.

"Fifty."

"Fifty! So is mine! And how rich is he? "

But it turned out they were just the same in that point; and though he cudgelled his brains to find out some difference, there seemed to be none; their kingdoms were exactly the same size, with exactly the same number of people in them, and their ancestors had been just as brave and glorious in peace or war. In fact, they were as like as two peas in a pod.

All this time the horses were champing their bits and pawing the ground, as if they would like to jump over each other's heads; and I daresay the Kings were getting impatient too, though they were much too dignified to say anything. And there they might have stayed till doomsday, but that King Godfrey's coachman hit on a fine idea. He suggested that perhaps one of them was a better King than the other; what were his master's virtues, would the other coachman kindly tell him?

The other coachman had his answer all ready, in poetry too, and this it was:

"Rough to the rough, my mighty King the mild with mildness sways,

Masters the good by goodness, and the bad with badness pays.

Give place, give place, O driver! such are this monarch's ways!"

"H'm," said King Godfrey's driver, "tit for tat is all very well, but I shouldn't call it *virtue* to pay out a bad man in his own coin."

"Oh, well," says the other in a huff, "you can call it *vice* if you like; and I should be very glad to hear all your King's *virtues*, if you laugh at mine!"

"Certainly," said King Godfrey's coachman; and, not to be beaten, he did his answer into poetry, like the other:

"He conquers wrath by mildness, the bad with goodness sways,

By gifts the miser vanquishes and lies with truth repays.

Give place, give place, O driver! such are this monarch's ways!"

Then the other man felt he had met his match. "I can't cap that," said he; "your master is better than mine." And the new King, who had not said a word all this time, thought it was time to be moving; perhaps he had been asleep; anyhow, he was not at all angry with his coachman, but out he got, and they let the horses loose, and pulled the carriage up on the slope to let King Godfrey pass by. But King Godfrey, before he went on, gave the other King a little good advice, which the King promised to take; for in that strange country people used to follow good advice sometimes. And then they said "Good-bye," and both went back home again, and both of them ruled their countries well until they died. The other King, we may be sure, was all the better for that lesson; and I hope Godfrey did not become conceited in that strange country, as he would have been if he lived here with us.

FINIS

www.ingramcontent.com/pod-product-compliance
Lightning Source LLC
Chambersburg PA
CBHW051306270626
PP18498200001B/2